FEARING THE UNKNOWN

"THE OLDEST AND STRONGEST KIND OF FEAR IS FEAR OF THE UNKNOWN"
H.P LOVECRAFT

MUSAIB MANZOOR

Copyright © Musaib Manzoor
All Rights Reserved.

This book has been published with all efforts taken to make the material error-free after the consent of the author. However, the author and the publisher do not assume and hereby disclaim any liability to any party for any loss, damage, or disruption caused by errors or omissions, whether such errors or omissions result from negligence, accident, or any other cause.

While every effort has been made to avoid any mistake or omission, this publication is being sold on the condition and understanding that neither the author nor the publishers or printers would be liable in any manner to any person by reason of any mistake or omission in this publication or for any action taken or omitted to be taken or advice rendered or accepted on the basis of this work. For any defect in printing or binding the publishers will be liable only to replace the defective copy by another copy of this work then available.

"The mosters that rose from the dead, they are nothing compared to the ones we carry in our hearts".

Contents

Preface

FEARING THE UNKNOWN
"THE OLDEST AND STRONGEST KIND OF FEAR IS
FEAR OF THE UNKNOWN"
H.P Lovecraft

My Paranormal Encounter

I always feel that there is something some kind of energy watching me.

And sometimes I even think that the objects in my room are staring at me.

Honestly I get freaked out well, probably everyone will get.

I think you all are thinking how is this possible? Is out of his mind right, well the answer is no.

I'm not out of my mind but the meaning of PARANORMAL Is not scientifically explainable.

So you can consider it as a yes too.

The night I started writing this book was the worst night off my life.

I heard voices, noises and someone was knocking on my door and windows.

So here are some stories that i wrote hope you will enjoy them.

ONE
MY SLEEP PARALYSIS

It happens every time I fall asleep on my back. I wake up and I can't tell if my eyes are open or shut, but I can "see" my whole room.

A dark presence is lurking on top of my wardrobe, and as soon as I notice it I try and scream, but I can't scream, and I can't move.

The darkness slithers down the side of my wardrobe, across the floor and looms over the end of my bed.

Then it creeps all over me, trying to invade every orifice.

I feel an immense pressure like it has pinned me down and is pushing its way into my ears, eyes, and mouth.

The darkness then screams a terrible screech into my face and I try to scream back until eventually I manage to jerk my head and everything disappears, and I'm alone in the darkness.

It is the most terrifying of experiences!

TWO
THE GRANDFATHER

My grandfather told me this story about how one time he was sitting in a chair in front of the house, when he heard his wife repeatedly calling him from inside the house.

The thing is, my grandmother passed away a few years before that.

But he told me that the voice was so pressing that he actually got up to look inside the house.

And as soon as he got inside he heard a loud crash behind him and turned around to see what happened.

The chair he has been sitting in moments ago had been crushed by the cast iron gutter that fell on it.

If he hadn't come inside the house he would have probably been seriously injured.

I don't know if it's paranormal or not, but everytime i think about it, it sends chills down my spine.

THREE

GONE TOWN

Liam a 16 year old boy from Almagro, Spain was living a happy life.

He was good in his studies and sports and was a fond of video games.

On 31th of July on a sunny day he was playing video games on his computer after a hour A bright lightning hits the Town Where he lives and the WiFi stoppes working then he goes outside to see what happened.

He looks at the street which was empty he gets shocked he goes a little further and arrives at a shop and no one was there, everyone has disappeared and now he is alone in that town.

He wonders where everyone has gone after a while he sees a dog staring at him with anger like he did everything, he runs back to his home in fear, now that poor boy is thinking what should I do, he calls his mother but her phone was switched off.

Somehow he spends a night next day he was in his living room crying, shouting for help,and he heard banging upstairs, so he went to see what it was.

He looked in all of the rooms he went back downstairs and lights all went out and it freaked him out, he tries to turn on the lamp but it won't turn on. He hears footsteps upstairs he walks up the stairs quietly.

he wants to see if anyone is really in his house right when he makes it up to the stairs he sees a dark figure at the end of the hall holding a knife, he screams and runs down the stairs and the dark figure was chasing after him and after a few seconds it disappeared.

He walked towards his house back walking out into the same hall to go to the bathroom.

On the same night, he awoke and felt the need to relieve himself.

He walked out from the room and distinctly heard the "look" and to my astonishment, a red light, almost like a spotlight was cast upon the wall at the very bottom of the stairs, the light had no other source, it was by itself. That's when he heard a very strong, masculine voice, completely strange.It said "stop! Right now go back to your room" He listened, turned around, and what happened next.

After reaching at the top of the stairs, he heard a very loud CRASH that sent him running back to his bed where he jumped straight under the covers and stayed there the whole night, when he woke up everything was normal, his family members were with him and it was the same day 31/ 07.

So was it just a bad dream no on that same day something *horrible* happened again.

The black figure appeared in front of everyone in that town at the same time and killed everyone including Liam it was another dream when he saw outside of the window there was no one and the Town was really gone.

FOUR
SATURDAY

When i was in the 12th grade,I had a friend called jessica in the school her life was full of problems family problems,boy and study problems.

When she came back to the school after the holidays,she started behaving strangely.She was very emotional She'd laugh one moment and cry the next.

I know something was very weird,the next day we had a math exam we studied through the night, on the terrace.

In the morning, a friend called me do you know what she said? Jessica had committed suicide.

I couldn't sleep a wink that night I kept staring at the ceiling fan, have you ever seen a suicide victim's body? bulging eyes a protruding Tongue and a broken neck.I still remember that night.

Saturday 13th of June those were my last few days at the School.

I was asleep one night And then all of a sudden, I woke up you know what I saw? Jessica.

As a ghost she was sitting by my feet staring at me.

Then she sat there for a while and then she left since then, she visits me every Saturday.

FIVE

LEMON CAKE

I've been staring at this menu for the last five minutes. I don't recognize any of the food items. They all seem like made-up words to me.

There are no pictures either. I don't know why James brought me to this restaurant.

It's my birthday today so he wanted to surprise me.

I appreciate it, but he could have picked a better place. He went here last week with his coworkers and loved it.

I really question his taste sometimes. There is nothing special about this place. All the walls have this disgusting brown color. The atmosphere is so depressing. Not to mention that there's barely anyone here.

"You can stop staring at the menu Susan. You know I'm gonna order for you," he says.

"Was just trying to figure things out," I reply.

"It's confusing. I get it, but trust me, the food here is delicious. Look, the waitress is on her way."

A tall skinny blonde woman comes by. She looks like she wants to be somewhere else. Honestly, I don't blame her.

"You're all ready to order?" she says apathetically.

"Yes, we'll both have number 20 please," says James.

She grabs our menus and walks away.

"What did you get us?" I ask.

"You'll see," he replies.

To my surprise, the waitress is already back. She gave each of us a piece of lemon cake.

"Enjoy," she says as she walks away.

"Happy birthday," says James.

"Thanks."

Did he just brought me here to eat lemon cake? I mean, it's my favorite. It looks good, but why are we starting with dessert? Something doesn't feel quite right.

"Aren't you gonna try it?" says James Impatiently.

"I will, it's just..."

"What's wrong?" he asks.

I see people from other tables looking at me. They all have a look of disgust on their face. The restaurant seems more crowded all of the sudden. Seats that were empty before are now occupied. Where did these people come from? What's their problem?

To make things worst, they started whispering. I can't understand what they're saying, but it's getting louder and louder. James doesn't seem bothered by any of this. In fact, he starts repeating himself. "Aren't you gonna try it?"

I'm just there staring at the lemon cake, looking away from everyone. I'm trying to ignore the whispers, but it's becoming unbearable. I want to get this over with, so I grab a bite.

The whispering stops. It got so quiet; you could hear the tiniest noise. Everybody in the restaurant, including James, is waiting for my verdict.

"So how is it? Do you like it?" James asks.

I feel sick. I get up and run towards the restroom. The people around me got angry and started calling me names

I've never heard of before.

As soon as I open the door, I started vomiting. What kind of cake was that?

Someone knocks on the door. "Is everything alright?" James shouts.

"I'm fine, just give me a moment." My stomach is turning. My throat hurts really bad as well. I've never felt this awful before. At least for now I'm away from all the chaos.

A couple of minutes went by. I can't say exactly how long. Was it 10 minutes, 15 minutes, or 20 minutes? Regardless, I feel a little bit better now. I no longer hear anything. Things seem calmer now.

After finally collecting myself, I open the door. I notice that everyone's gone, except for James. Strangely, his head is on the table, as if he was taking a nap. Half of his lemon cake is eaten. I'm slowly making my way back. As I get closer, I see that his eyes are wide open. Blood was coming out of his mouth.

"James!?" I panic. He's not moving. I started screaming. "Is anybody here!? I need help!"

I yell multiple times, hoping there would be someone to hear me. Nobody is answering. I'm looking for my phone but then I remember that I left it in the car. Suddenly, gas was coming from the kitchen. The smell is terrible. I quickly run to the exit door, but it's locked. I started to feel dizzy. I'm trying to find another door, but the atmosphere is getting more and more suffocating. Next thing I know, I'm on the ground. I can't feel my body. Everything is pitch black. I can barely open my eyes. There seems to be some people around me. It's hard to look at their faces since my vision is somewhat blurred. How long was I asleep for?

"This is the patient you'll be helping us to take care of."

Who is this woman? What's going on? What is this place? Wait, I think I'm getting my vision back.

"What happened?"

"She just had another episode."

"We've been trying all kinds of medications for months; they don't seem to work."

Is that...the waitress? Why is she wearing a doctor's uniform? The others...they seem like nurses.

"Her condition has gotten worse since we brought her here."

"What are we going to do?"

"I don't know."

"They should have sent her to prison for what she did to her husband. She Doesn't belong here."

"What did she do?"

"She poisoned him."

Poison? I didn't poison James. No no, she got it all wrong.

"Let's bring her back to her room, we'll see what else we can do tomorrow."

I'm trying to speak, but I can't. Are these side effects? Who knows what they've put in my body. I need to get out of here. Why are they saying that I poisoned my husband? I would never do that. I need to find the real killer.

They brough me into this dark room with no windows. The door shuts abruptly and now I'm all alone. I'm attached to this bed, and I can barely move.

I need to get out of here. I need answers. I'll try closing my eyes and think. I have to remember what happened. Who put poison in the lemon cake?

SIX

I REGULARLY SAW A GIRL THAT WAS PINK AND SEE THROUGH

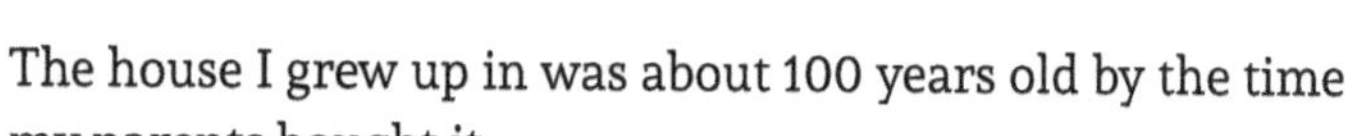

The house I grew up in was about 100 years old by the time my parents bought it.

I lived there until I was 16. For as long as I can remember, I saw what I described as 'a girl that was pink and see through.'

I always called her Pam. It's been 10 years since I lived in that house and I still remember her vividly.

My dad got a bit weirded out when I would talk about Pam and finally when I was 13, my mom put me in therapy because Pam was still something I brought up regularly.

In order to stop my parents from thinking I was crazy, I just stopped talking about Pam completely and went on with life.

That was until my parents decided to put the house up for sale when I was 16.

Just two weeks before moving into our new house, I was sleeping, but was woken up by Pam standing in my doorway and pointing into the bathroom that was directly across the hall.

All Pam said was 'look, my mom.' And when I looked to see who she was pointing at, I saw a woman hanging by a cord from the light fixture in the bathroom.

I remember the woman looked as though she had been hanging there for a while, when all of a sudden the woman's boot fell off and I abruptly woke up.

I ran into my parents room to tell them what happened, and my mom looked at me disappointed because I was taking about Pam again after having kept quiet about her for years. I concluded that it was just a bad dream and went back to bed with no other incidences.

Until a few days later. I was once again asleep, and dreaming that I was woken up by crying coming from the bathroom across the hall.

I got out of bed and walked over to see what was going on.

At that point, I saw the same woman that was hanging from the bathroom light fixture, sobbing and holding a very real little girl under the water in the bathtub.

It was then that I realized that the little girl was the little pink see through girl I had seen my entire life.

It was Pam. And she was not moving.

I immediately woke up and I was crying uncontrollably. I was 16 years old, and I ran into my parents room like a 5 year old, and jumped into bed with my mom (my dad was working at the time).

I told my mom what had happened and my mom could see how upset I was and was trying to calm me down.

At that same moment, the pink and transparent version of Pam walked through the door.

I looked at my mom and just whispered, 'oh my god mom. She's in here' and I pulled the covers up to my neck and just looked at my mom terrified.

My mom was speechless. At that point, Pam slowly walked up the side of the bed and began shoving me into my mom.

I had never been touched by Pam before. I was screaming and crying and kept yelling 'STOP TOUCHING ME!'

And all that my mom could reply was 'I'm not touching you!' As she was being pushed out of the other side of the bed.

After what seemed like forever, Pam stopped and slowly walked out of the room.

I cried myself to sleep, and my mom stayed awake to see what else would happen.

I never spent another night in that house.

But, two weeks after we moved out completely, the house caught fire.

The entire back side as well as the entire garage burnt. The official cause was 'spontaneous combustion.'

The house that my family lived in for 25 years has since been bought and sold 8 times within 10 years. No one wants to stay in that house, and I really think that Pam is the reason why.

SEVEN
THE RAVEN

Once upon a midnight dreary, while I pondered, weak and weary,

Over many a quaint and curious volume of forgotten lore,

While I nodded, nearly napping, suddenly there came a tapping,

As of some one gently rapping, rapping at my chamber door.

"'Tis some visitor," I muttered, "tapping at my chamber door –

Only this, and nothing more."

Ah, distinctly I remember it was in the bleak December,

And each separate dying ember wrought its ghost upon the floor.

Eagerly I wished the morrow; - vainly I had sought to borrow

From my books surcease of sorrow – sorrow for the lost Lenore –

For the rare and radiant maiden whom the angels name Lenore –

Nameless here for evermore.

And the silken sad uncertain rustling of each purple curtain
Thrilled me – filled me with fantastic terrors never felt before;
So that now, to still the beating of my heart, I stood repeating
"'Tis some visitor entreating entrance at my chamber door –
Some late visitor entreating entrance at my chamber door; -
This it is, and nothing more."
Presently my soul grew stronger; hesitating then no longer,
"Sir," said I, "or Madam, truly your forgiveness I implore;
But the fact is I was napping, and so gently you came rapping,
And so faintly you came tapping, tapping at my chamber door,
That I scarce was sure I heard you " – here I opened wide the door; -
Darkness there and nothing more.
Deep into that darkness peering, long I stood there wondering, fearing,
Doubting, dreaming dreams no mortal ever dared to dream before;
But the silence was unbroken, and the darkness gave no token,
And the only word there spoken was the whispered word, "Lenore!"
This I whispered, and an echo murmured back the word, "Lenore!" –
Merely this, and nothing more.

Back into the chamber turning, all my soul within me burning,

Soon I heard again a tapping somewhat louder than before.

"Surely," said I, "surely that is something at my window lattice;

Let me see, then, what thereat is, and this mystery explore –

Let my heart be still a moment and this mystery explore;-

'Tis the wind and nothing more!"

Open here I flung the shutter, when, with many a flirt and flutter,

In there stepped a stately raven of the saintly days of yore;

Not the least obeisance made he; not an instant stopped or stayed he;

But, with mien of lord or lady, perched above my chamber door –

Perched upon a bust of Pallas just above my chamber door –

Perched, and sat, and nothing more.

Then this ebony bird beguiling my sad fancy into smiling,

By the grave and stern decorum of the countenance it wore,

"Though thy crest be shorn and shaven, thou," I said, "art sure no craven,

Ghastly grim and ancient raven wandering from the Nightly shore –

Tell me what thy lordly name is on the Night's Plutonian shore!"

Quoth the raven "Nevermore."

Much I marvelled this ungainly fowl to hear discourse so plainly,
    Though its answer little meaning – little relevancy bore;
    For we cannot help agreeing that no living human being
    Ever yet was blessed with seeing bird above his chamber door –
    Bird or beast upon the sculptured bust above his chamber door,
        With such name as "Nevermore."

But the raven, sitting lonely on the placid bust, spoke only
    That one word, as if his soul in that one word he did outpour.
    Nothing farther then he uttered – not a feather then he fluttered –
    Till I scarcely more than muttered "Other friends have flown before –
    On the morrow he will leave me, as my hopes have flown before."
        Then the bird said "Nevermore."

Startled at the stillness broken by reply so aptly spoken,
    "Doubtless," said I, "what it utters is its only stock and store
    Caught from some unhappy master whom unmerciful Disaster
    Followed fast and followed faster till his songs one burden bore –
    Till the dirges of his Hope that melancholy burden bore
        Of "Never – nevermore."

But the raven still beguiling all my sad soul into smiling,
    Straight I wheeled a cushioned seat in front of bird, and bust and door;
    Then, upon the velvet sinking, I betook myself to linking

Fancy unto fancy, thinking what this ominous bird of yore –
What this grim, ungainly, ghastly, gaunt and ominous bird of yore
Meant in croaking "Nevermore."
This I sat engaged in guessing, but no syllable expressing
To the fowl whose fiery eyes now burned into my bosom's core;
This and more I sat divining, with my head at ease reclining
On the cushion's velvet lining that the lamplight gloated o'er,
But whose velvet violet lining with the lamplight gloating o'er,
She shall press, ah, nevermore!
Then, me-thought, the air grew denser, perfumed from an unseen censer
Swung by Angels whose faint foot-falls tinkled on the tufted floor.
"Wretch," I cried, "thy God hath lent thee – by these angels he hath sent
Thee
Respite – respite and nepenthe from thy memories of Lenore;
Quaff, oh quaff this kind nepenthe and forget this lost Lenore!"
Quoth the raven, "Nevermore."
"Prophet!" said I, "thing of evil! – prophet still, if bird or devil! –
Whether Tempter sent, or whether tempest tossed thee here ashore,
Desolate yet all undaunted, on this desert land enchanted –

On this home by Horror haunted – tell me truly, I implore –

Is there – is there balm in Gilead? – tell me – tell me, I implore!"

Quoth the raven, "Nevermore."

"Prophet!" said I, "thing of evil – prophet still, if bird or devil!

By that Heaven that bends above us – by that God we both adore –

Tell this soul with sorrow laden if, within the distant Aidenn,

It shall clasp a sainted maiden whom the angels name Lenore –

Clasp a rare and radiant maiden whom the angels name Lenore."

Quoth the raven, "Nevermore."

"Be that word our sign of parting, bird or fiend!" I shrieked, up-starting –

"Get thee back into the tempest and the Night's Plutonian shore!

Leave no black plume as a token of that lie thy soul hath spoken!

Leave my loneliness unbroken! – quit the bust above my door!

Take thy beak from out my heart, and take thy form from off my door!"

Quoth the raven, "Nevermore."

And the raven, never flitting, still is sitting, still is sitting

On the pallid bust of Pallas just above my chamber door;

And his eyes have all the seeming of a demon's that is dreaming,

And the lamp-light o'er him streaming throws his shadow on the floor;

And my soul from out that shadow that lies floating on
the floor
    Shall be lifted – nevermore!

EIGHT

THE SILENT WOMAN

The uproarious merriment of a wedding-feast burst forth into the night from a brilliantly lighted house in the "gasse" (narrow street). It was one of those nights touched with the warmth of spring, but dark and full of soft mist. Most fitting it was for a celebration of the union of two yearning hearts to share the same lot, a lot that may possibly dawn in sunny brightness, but also become clouded and sullen—for a long, long time! But how merry and joyous they were over there, those people of the happy olden times! They, like us, had their troubles and trials, and when misfortune visited them it came not to them with soft cushions and tender pressures of the hand. Rough and hard, with clinched fist, it laid hold upon them. But when they gave vent to their happy feelings and sought to enjoy themselves, they were like swimmers in cooling waters. They struck out into the stream with freshness and courage, suffered themselves to be borne along by the current whithersoever it took its course. This was the cause of such a jubilee, such a thoughtlessly noisy outburst of all kinds of soul-possessing gayety from this house of nuptials.

"And if I had known," the bride's father, the rich Ruben Klattaner, had just said, "that it would take the last gulden in my pocket, then out it would have come."

In fact, it did appear as if the last groschen had really taken flight, and was fluttering about in the form of platters heaped up with geese and pastry-tarts. Since two o'clock—that is, since the marriage ceremony had been performed out

in the open street—until nearly midnight, the wedding-feast had been progressing, and even yet the sarvers, or waiters, were hurrying from room to room. It was as if a twofold blessing had descended upon all this abundance of food and drink, for, in the first place, they did not seem to diminish; secondly, they ever found a new place for disposal. To be sure, this appetite was sharpened by the presence of a little dwarf-like, unimportant-looking man. He was esteemed, however, none the less highly by every one. They had specially written to engage the celebrated "Leb Narr," of Prague. And when was ever a mood so out of sorts, a heart so imbittered as not to thaw out and laugh if Leb Narr played one of his pranks. Ah, thou art now dead, good fool! Thy lips, once always ready with a witty reply, are closed. Thy mouth, then never still, now speaks no more! But when the hearty peals of laughter once rang forth at thy command, intercessors, as it were, in thy behalf before the very throne of God, thou hadst nothing to fear. And the joy of that "other" world was thine, that joy that has ever belonged to the most pious of country rabbis!

In the mean time the young people had assembled in one of the rooms to dance. It was strange how the sound of violins and trumpets accorded with the drolleries of the wit from Prague. In one part the outbursts of merriment were so boisterous that the very candles on the little table seemed to flicker with terror; in another an ordinary conversation was in progress, which now and then only ran over into a loud tittering, when some old lady slipped into the circle and tried her skill at a redowa, then altogether unknown to the young people. In the very midst of the tangle of dancers was to be seen the bride in a heavy silk wedding-gown. The point of her golden hood hung far down over her face. She danced continuously. She danced with every one that asked her. Had one, however,

observed the actions of the young woman, they would certainly have seemed to him hurried, agitated, almost wild. She looked no one in the eye, not even her own bridegroom. He stood for the most part in the door-way, and evidently took more pleasure in the witticisms of the fool than in the dance or the lady dancers. But who ever thought for a moment why the young woman's hand burned, why her breath was so hot when one came near to her lips? Who should have noticed so strange a thing? A low whispering already passed through the company, a stealthy smile stole across many a lip. A bevy of ladies was seen to enter the room suddenly. The music dashed off into one of its loudest pieces, and, as if by enchantment, the newly made bride disappeared behind the ladies. The bridegroom, with his stupid, smiling mien, was still left standing on the threshold. But it was not long before he too vanished. One could hardly say how it happened. But people understand such skillful movements by experience, and will continue to understand them as long as there are brides and grooms in the world.

This disappearance of the chief personages, little as it seemed to be noticed, gave, however, the signal for general leave-taking. The dancing became drowsy; it stopped all at once, as if by appointment. That noisy confusion now began which always attends so merry a wedding-party. Half-drunken voices could be heard still intermingled with a last, hearty laugh over a joke of the fool from Prague echoing across the table. Here and there some one, not quite sure of his balance, was fumbling for the arm of his chair or the edge of the table. This resulted in his overturning a dish that had been forgotten, or in spilling a beer-glass. While this, in turn, set up a new hubbub, some one else, in his eagerness to betake himself from the scene, fell flat into the very débris. But all this tumult was really hushed

the moment they all pressed to the door, for at that very instant shrieks, cries of pain, were heard issuing from the entrance below. In an instant the entire outpouring crowd with all possible force pushed back into the room, but it was a long time before the stream was pressed back again. Meanwhile, painful cries were again heard from below, so painful, indeed, that they restored even the most drunken to a state of consciousness.

"By the living God!" they cried to each other, "what is the matter down there? Is the house on fire?"

"She is gone! She is gone!" shrieked a woman's voice from the entry below.

"Who? Who?" groaned the wedding-guests, seized, as it were, with an icy horror.

"Gone! Gone!" cried the woman from the entry, and hurrying up the stairs came Selde Klattaner, the mother of the bride, pale as death, her eyes dilated with most awful fright, convulsively grasping a candle in her hand. "For God's sake, what has happened?" was heard on every side of her.

The sight of so many people about her, and the confusion of voices, seemed to release the poor woman

from a kind of stupor. She glanced shyly about her then,
as if overcome with a sense of shame stronger than her terror, andsaid, in a suppressed tone:

"Nothing, nothing, good people. In God's name, I ask, what was there to happen?"

Dissimulation, however, was too evident to suffice to deceive them.

"Why, then, did you shriek so, Selde," called out one of the guests to her, "if nothing happened?"

"Yes, she has gone," Selde now moaned in heart-rending tones, "and she has certainly done herself some harm!"

The cause of this strange scene was now first discovered. The bride has disappeared from the wedding-feast. Soon after that she had vanished in such a mysterious way, the bridegroom went below to the dimly-lighted room to find her, but in vain. At first thought this seemed to him to be a sort of bashful jest; but not finding her here, a mysterious foreboding seized him. He called to the mother of the bride:

"Woe to me! This woman has gone!"

Presently this party, that had so admirably controlled itself, was again thrown into commotion. "There was nothing to do," was said on all sides, "but to ransack every nook and corner. Remarkable instances of such disappearances of brides had been known. Evil spirits were wont to lurk about such nights and to inflict mankind with all sorts of sorceries." Strange as this explanation may seem, there were many who believed it at this very moment, and, most of all, Selde Klattaner herself. But it was only for a moment, for she at once exclaimed:

"No, no, my good people, she is gone; I know she is gone!"

Now for the first time many of them, especially the mothers, felt particularly uneasy, and anxiously called their daughters to them. Only a few showed courage, and urged that they must search and search, even if they had to turn aside the river Iser a hundred times. They urgently pressed on, called for torches and lanterns, and started forth. The cowardly ran after them up and down the stairs. Before any one perceived it the room was entirely forsaken.

Ruben Klattaner stood in the hall entry below, and let the people hurry past him without exchanging a word with any. Bitter disappointment and fear had almost crazed him. One of the last to stay in the room above with Selde was, strange to

say, Leb Narr, of Prague. After all had departed, he approached the miserable mother, and, in a tone least becoming his general manner, inquired:

"Tell me, now, Mrs. Selde, did she not wish to have 'him'?"

"Whom? Whom?" cried Selde, with renewed alarm, when she found herself alone with the fool.

"I mean," said Leb, in a most sympathetic manner, approaching still nearer to Selde, "that maybe you had to make your daughter marry him."

"Make? And have we, then, made her?" moaned Selde, staring at the fool with a look of uncertainty.

"Then nobody needs to search for her," replied the fool, with a sympathetic laugh, at the same time retreating. "It's better to leave her where she is."

Without saying thanks or good-night, he was gone.

Meanwhile the cause of all this disturbance had arrived at the end of her flight.

Close by the synagogue was situated the house of the rabbi. It was built in an angle of a very narrow street, set in a framework of tall shade-trees. Even by daylight it was dismal enough. At night it was almost impossible for a timid person to approach it, for people declared that the low supplications of the dead could be heard in the dingy house of God when at night they took the rolls of the law from the ark to summon their members by name.

Through this retired street passed, or rather ran, at this hour a shy form. Arriving at the dwelling of the rabbi, she glanced backward to see whether any one was following her. But all was silent and gloomy enough about her. A pale light issued from one of the windows of the synagogue; it came from the "eternal lamp" hanging in front of the ark of the covenant. But at this moment it seemed to her as if a supernatural eye was gazing upon her. Thoroughly affrighted, she seized the little iron knocker of the door and struck it gently. But the throb of her beating heart was even louder, more violent, than this blow. After a pause, footsteps were heard passing slowly along the hallway.

The rabbi had not occupied this lonely house a long time. His predecessor, almost a centenarian in years, had been laid to rest a few months before. The new rabbi had been called, from a distant part of the country. He was unmarried, and in the prime of life. No one had known him before his coming. But his personal nobility and the profundity of his scholarship made up for his deficiency in years. An aged

mother had accompanied him from their distant home, and she took the place of wife and child.

"Who is there?" asked the rabbi, who had been busy at his desk even at this late hour and thus had not missed hearing the knocker.

"It is I," the figure without responded, almost inaudibly.

"Speak louder, if you wish me to hear you," replied the rabbi.

"It is I, Ruben Klattaner's daughter," she repeated.

The name seemed to sound strange to the rabbi. He as yet knew too few of his congregation to understand that this very day he performed the marriage ceremony of the person who had just repeated her name. Therefore he called out, after a moment's pause, "What do you wish so late at night?"

"Open the door, rabbi," she answered, pleadingly, "or I shall die at once!"

The bolt was pushed back. Something gleaming, rustling, glided past the rabbi into the dusky hall. The light of the candle in his hand was not sufficient to allow

him to descry it. Before he had time to address her, she had vanished past him and had disappeared through the open door into the room. Shaking his head, the rabbi again bolted the door.

On re entering the room he saw a woman's form sitting in the chair which he usually occupied. She had her back turned to him. Her head was bent low over her breast. Her golden wedding-hood, with its shading lace, was pulled down over her forehead. Courageous and pious as the rabbi was, he could not rid himself of a feeling of terror.

"Who are you?" he demanded, in a loud tone, as if its sound alone would banish the presence of this being that seemed to him at this moment to be the production of all the enchantments of evil spirits.

She raised herself, and cried in a voice that seemed to come from the agony of a human being:

"Do you not know me—me, whom you married a few hours since under the chuppe (marriage-canopy) to a husband?"

On hearing this familiar voice the rabbi stood speechless. He gazed at the young woman. Now, indeed, he must regard her as one bereft of reason, rather than as a specter.

"Well, if you are she," he stammered out, after a pause, for it was with difficulty that he found words to answer, "why are you here and not in the place where you belong?"

"I know no other place to which I belong more than here where I now am!" she answered, severely.

These words puzzled the rabbi still more. Is it really an insane woman before him? He must have thought so, for he now addressed her in a gentle tone of voice, as we do those suffering from this kind of sickness, in order not to excite her, and said:

"The place where you belong, my daughter, is in the house of your parents, and, since you have to-day been made a wife, your place is in your husband's house."

The young woman muttered something which failed to reach the rabbi's ear. Yet he only continued to think that he saw before him some poor unfortunate whose mind was deranged. After a pause, he added, in a still gentler tone: "What is your name, then, my child?"

"God, god," she moaned, in the greatest anguish, "he does not even yet know my name!"

"How should I know you," he continued, apologetically, "for I am a stranger in this place?"

This tender remark seemed to have produced the desired effect upon her excited mind.

"My name is Veile," she said, quietly, after a pause.

The rabbi quickly perceived that he had adopted the right tone towards his mysterious guest.

"Veile," he said, approaching nearer her, "what do you wish of me?"

"Rabbi, I have a great sin resting heavily upon my heart," she replied despondently. "I do not know what to do."

"What can you have done," inquired the rabbi, with a tender look, "that cannot be discussed at any other time than just now? Will you let me advise you, Veile?"

"No, no," she cried again, violently, "I will not be advised. I see, I know what oppresses me. Yes, I can grasp it by the hand, it lies so near before me. Is that what you call to be advised?"

"Very well," returned the rabbi, seeing that this was the very way to get the young woman to talk—"very well, I say, you are not imagining anything. I believe that you have greatly sinned. Have you come here then to confess this sin? Do your parents or your husband know anything about it?"

"Who is my husband?" she interrupted him, impetuously.

Thoughts welled up in the rabbi's heart like a tumultuous sea in which opposing conjectures cross and recross each other's course. Should he speak with her as with an ordinary sinner?

"Were you, perhaps, forced to be married?" he inquired, as quietly as possible, after a pause.

A suppressed sob, a strong inward struggle, manifesting itself in the whole trembling body, was the only answer to this question.

"Tell me, my child," said the rabbi, encouragingly.

In such tones as the rabbi had never before heard, so strange, so surpassing any human sounds, the young woman began:

"Yes, rabbi, I will speak, even though I know that I shall never go from this place alive, which would be the very best thing for me! No, rabbi, I was not forced to be married. My parents have never once said to me 'you must,' but my own will, my own desire, rather, has always been supreme. My husband is the son of a rich man in the community. To enter his family was to be made the first lady in the gasse, to sit buried in gold and silver. And that very thing, nothing else, was what infatuated me with him. It was for that that I forced myself, my heart and will, to be married to him, hard as it was for me. But in my innermost heart I detested him. The more he loved me, the more I hated him. But the gold and silver had an influence over me. More and more they cried to me, 'You will be the first lady in the gasse!'"

"Continue," said the rabbi, when she ceased, almost exhausted by these words.

"What more shall I tell you, rabbi?" she began again. "I was never a liar, when a child, or older, and yet during my whole engagement it has seemed to me as if a big, gigantic lie had followed me step by step. I have seen it on every side of me. But to-day, when I stood under the chuppe, rabbi, and he took the ring from his finger and put it on mine, and when I had to dance at my own wedding with him, whom I now recognized, now for the first time, as the lie, and—when they led me away——"

This sincere confession escaping from the lips of the young woman, she sobbed aloud and bowed her head still deeper over her breast. The rabbi gazed upon her in silence. No insane woman ever spoke like that! Only a soul conscious of its own sin, but captivated by a mysterious power, could suffer like this!

It was not sympathy which he felt with her; it was much more a living over the sufferings of the woman. In spite of the confused story, it was all clear to the rabbi. The cause of the flight from the father's house at this hour also required no explanation. "I know what you mean," he longed to say, but he could only find words to say: "Speak further, Veile!"

The young woman turned towards him. He had not yet seen her face. The golden hood with the shading lace hung deeply over it.

"Have I not told you everything?" she said, with a flush of scorn.

"Everything?" repeated the rabbi, inquiringly. He only said this, moreover, through embarrassment.

"Do you tell me now," she cried, at once passionately and mildly, "what am I to do?"

"Veile!" exclaimed the rabbi, entertaining now, for the first time, a feeling of repugnance for this confidential interview.

"Tell me now!" she pleaded; and before the rabbi could prevent it the young woman threw herself down at his feet and clasped his knees in her arms. This hasty act had loosened the golden wedding-hood from her head, and thus exposed her face to view, a face of remarkable beauty.

So overcome was the young rabbi by the sight of it that he had to shade his eyes with his hands, as if before a sudden flash of lightning.

"Tell me now, what shall I do?" she cried again. "Do you think that I have come from my parents' home merely to return again without help? You alone in the

world must tell me. Look at me! I have kept all my hair just as God gave it me. It has never been touched by the shears. Should I, then, do anything to please my husband? I am no wife. I will not be a wife! Tell me, tell me, what am I to do?"

"Arise, arise," bade the rabbi; but his voice quivered, sounded almost painful.

"Tell me first," she gasped; "I will not rise till then!"

"How can I tell you?" he moaned, almost inaudibly.

"Naphtali!" shrieked the kneeling woman.

But the rabbi staggered backward. The room seemed ablaze before him, like a bright fire. A sharp cry rang from his breast, as if one suffering from some painful wound had been seized by a rough hand. In his hurried attempt to free himself from the embrace of the young woman, who still clung to his knees, it chanced that her head struck heavily against the floor.

"Naphtali!" she cried once again.

"Silence, silence," groaned the rabbi, pressing both hands against his head.

And still again she called out this name, but not with that agonizing cry. It sounded rather like a commingling of exultation and lamentation.

And again he demanded, "Silence! Silence!" but this time so imperiously, so forcibly, that the young woman lay on the floor as if conjured, not daring to utter a single word.

The rabbi paced almost wildly up and down the room. There must have been a hard, terrible struggle in his breast. It seemed to the one lying on the floor that she heard him sigh from the depths of his soul. Then his pacing became calmer; but it did not last long. The fierce conflict again assailed him. His step grew hurried; it echoed loudly through the awful stillness of the room. Suddenly he neared the young woman, who seemed to lie there scarcely breathing. He stopped in front of her. Had any one seen the face of the rabbi at this moment the expression on it would have filled him with terror. There was a marvelous tranquillity overlying it, the tranquillity of a struggle for life or death.

"Listen to me now, Veile," he began, slowly. "I will talk with you."

"I listen, rabbi," she whispered.

"But do you hear me well?"

"Only speak," she returned.

"But will you do what I advise you? Will you not oppose it? For I am going to say something that will terrify you."

"I will do anything that you say. Only tell me," she moaned.

"Will you swear?"

"I will," she groaned.

"No, do not swear yet, until you have heard me," he cried. "I will not force you."

This time came no answer.

"Hear me, then, daughter of Ruben Klattaner," he began, after a pause. "You have a twofold sin upon your soul, and each is so great, so criminal, that it can only be forgiven by severe punishment. First you permitted yourself to be infatuated by

the gold and silver, and then you forced your heart to lie. With the lie you sought to deceive the man, even though he had intrusted you with his all when he made you his wife. A lie is truly a great sin! Streams of water cannot drown them. They make men false and hateful to themselves. The worst that has been committed in the world was led in by a lie. That is the one sin."

"I know, I know," sobbed the young woman.

"Now hear me further," began the rabbi again, with a wavering voice, after a short pause. "You have committed a still greater sin than the first. You have not only deceived your husband, but you have also destroyed the happiness of another person. You could have spoken, and you did not. For life you have robbed him of his happiness, his light, his joy, but you did not speak. What can he now do, when he knows what has been lost to him?"

"Naphtali!" cried the young woman.

"Silence! Silence! Do not let that name pass your lips again," he demanded, violently. "The more you repeat it the greater becomes your sin. Why did you not speak when you could have spoken? God can never easily forgive you that.

To be silent, to keep secret in one's breast what would have made another man happier than the mightiest monarch! Thereby you have made him more than

unhappy. He will nevermore have the desire to be happy. Veile, God in heaven cannot forgive you for that."

"Silence! Silence!" groaned the wretched woman.

"No, Veile," he continued, with a stronger voice, "let me talk now. You are certainly willing to hear me speak? Listen to me. You must do severe penance for this sin, the twofold sin which rests upon your head. God is long-suffering and merciful. He will perhaps look down upon your misery, and will blot out your guilt from the great book of transgressions. But you must become penitent. Hear, now, what it shall be."

The rabbi paused. He was on the point of saying the severest thing that had ever passed his lips.

"You were silent, Veile," then he cried, "when you should have spoken. Be silent now forever to all men and to yourself. From the moment you leave this house, until I grant it, you must be dumb; you dare not let a loud word pass from your mouth. Will you undergo this penance?"

"I will do all you say," moaned the young woman.

"Will you have strength to do it?" he asked, gently.

"I shall be as silent as death," she replied.

"And one thing more I have to say to you," he continued. "You are the wife of your husband. Return home and be a Jewish wife."

"I understand you," she sobbed in reply.

"Go to your home now, and bring peace to your parents and husband. The time will come when you may speak, when your sin will be forgiven you. Till then bear what has been laid upon you."

"May I say one thing more?" she cried, lifting up her head.

"Speak," he said.

"Naphtali!"

The rabbi covered his eyes with one hand, with the other motioned her to be silent. But she grasped his hand, drew it to her lips. Hot tears fell upon it.

"Go now," he sobbed, completely broken down.

She let go the hand. The rabbi had seized the candle, but she had already passed him, and glided through the dark hall. The door was left open. The rabbi locked it again.

Veile returned to her home, as she had escaped, unnoticed. The narrow street was deserted, as desolate as death. The searchers were to be found everywhere except there where they ought first to have sought for the missing one. Her mother, Selde, still sat on the same chair on which she had sunk down an hour ago. The fright had left her like one paralyzed, and she was unable to rise. What a wonderful contrast this wedding-room, with the mother sitting alone in it, presented to the hilarity reigning here shortly before! On Veile's entrance her mother did not cry out. She had no strength to do so. She merely said: "So you have come at last, my daughter?" as if Veile had only returned from a walk somewhat too long. But the young woman did not answer to this and similar questions. Finally she signified by gesticulations that she could not speak. Fright seized the wretched mother a second time, and the entire house was filled with her lamentations.

Ruben Klattaner and Veile's husband having now returned from their fruitless search, were horrified on perceiving the change which Veile had undergone. Being men, they did not weep. With staring eyes they gazed upon the silent young woman, and beheld in her an apparition which had been dealt with by God's visitation in a mysterious manner.

From this hour began the terrible penance of the young woman.

The impression which Veile's woeful condition made upon the people of the gasse was wonderful. Those who had danced with her that evening on the wedding now first recalled her excited state. Her wild actions were now first remembered by many. It must have been an "evil eye," they concluded—a jealous, evil eye, to which her beauty was hateful. This alone could have possessed her with a demon of unrest. She was driven by this evil power into the dark night, a sport of these malicious potencies which pursue men step by step, especially on such occasions. The living God alone knows what she must have seen that night. Nothing good, else one would not become dumb. Old legends and tales were revived, each more horrible than the other. Hundreds of instances were given to prove that this was nothing new in the gasse. Despite this explanation, it is remarkable that the people did not believe that the young woman was dumb. The most thought that her power of speech had been paralyzed by some awful fright, but that with time it would be restored. Under this supposition they called her "Veile the Silent."

There is a kind of human eloquence more telling, more forcible than the loudest words, than the choicest diction—the silence of woman! Ofttimes they cannot endure the slightest vexation, but some great, heart-breaking sorrow, some pain from constant renunciation, self-sacrifice, they suffer with sealed lips—as if, in very truth, they were bound with bars of iron.

It would be difficult to fully describe that long "silent" life of the young woman. It is almost impossible to cite more than one incident. Veile accompanied her husband to his home, that house resplendent with that gold and silver which had infatuated her. She was, to be sure, the "first" woman in the gasse; she had everything in abundance. Indeed, the world supposed that she had but little cause for complaint. "Must one have everything?" was sometimes queried in the gasse. "One has one thing; another, another." And, according to all appearances, the people were right. Veile continued to be the beautiful, blooming woman. Her penance of silence did not deprive her of a single charm. She was so very happy, indeed, that she did not seem to feel even the pain of her punishment. Veile could laugh and rejoice, but never did she forget to be silent. The seemingly happy days, however, were only qualified to bring about the proper time of trials and temptations. The beginning was easy enough for her, the middle and end were times of real pain. The first years of their wedded life were childless. "It is well," the people in the gasse said, "that she has no children, and God has rightly ordained it to be so. A mother who cannot talk to her child, that would be something awful!" Unexpectedly to all, she rejoiced one day in the birth of a daughter. And when that affectionate young creature, her own offspring, was laid upon her breast, and the first sounds were uttered by its lips—that nameless, eloquent utterance of an infant—she forgot herself not; she was silent!

She was silent also when from day to day that child blossomed before her eyes into fuller beauty. Nor had she any words for it when, in effusions of tenderness, it stretched forth its tiny arms, when in burning fever it sought for the mother's hand. For days—yes, weeks—together she watched at its bedside. Sleep never visited her eyes. But she ever remembered her penance.

Years fled by. In her arms she carried another child. It was a boy. The father's joy was great. The child inherited its mother's beauty. Like its sister, it grew in health and strength. The noblest, richest mother, they said, might be proud of such children! And Veile was proud, no doubt, but this never passed her lips. She remained silent about things which mothers in their joy often cannot find words enough to express. And although her face many times lighted up with beaming smiles, yet she never renounced the habitual silence imposed upon her.

The idea that the slightest dereliction of her penance would be accompanied with a curse upon her children may have impressed itself upon her mind. Mothers will understand better than other persons what this mother suffered from her penalty of silence.

Thus a part of those years sped away which we are wont to call the best. She still flourished in her wonderful beauty. Her maiden daughter was beside her, like the bud beside the full-blown rose. Suitors were already present from far and near, who passed in review before the beautiful girl. The most of them were excellent

young men, and any mother might have been proud in having her own daughter sought by such. Even then Veile did not undo her penance. Those busy times of intercourse which keep mothers engaged in presenting the superiorities of their daughters in the best light were not allowed her. The choice of one of the most favored suitors was made. Never before did any couple in the gasse equal this in beauty and grace. A few weeks before the appointed time for the wedding a malignant disease stole on, spreading sorrow and anxiety over the greater part of the land. Young girls were principally its victims. It seemed to pass scornfully over the aged and infirm. Veile's daughter was also laid hold upon by it. Before three days had passed there was a corpse in the house—the bride!

Even then Veile did not forget her penance. When they bore away the corpse to the "good place," she did utter a cry of anguish which long after echoed in the ears of the people; she did wring her hands in despair, but no one heard a word of complaint. Her lips seemed dumb forever. It was then, when she was seated on the low stool in the seven days of mourning, that the rabbi came to her, to bring to her the usual consolation for the dead. But he did not speak with her. He addressed words only to her husband. She herself dared not look up. Only when he turned to go did she lift her eyes. They, in turn, met the eyes of the rabbi, but he departed without a farewell.

After her daughter's death Veile was completely broken down. Even that which at her time of life is still called beauty had faded away within a few days. Her cheeks had become hollow, her hair gray. Visitors wondered how she could endure such a shock, how body and spirit could hold together. They did not know that that silence was an iron fetter firmly imprisoning the slumbering spirits. She had a son, moreover, to whom, as to something last and dearest, her whole being still clung.

The boy was thirteen years old. His learning in the Holy Scriptures was already celebrated for miles around. He was the pupil of the rabbi, who had treated him with a love and tenderness becoming his own father. He said that he was a remarkable child, endowed with rare talents. The boy was to be sent to Hungary, to one of the most celebrated teachers of the times, in order to lay the foundation for his sacred studies under this instructor's guidance and wisdom. Years might perhaps pass before she would see him again. But Veile let her boy go from her embrace. She did not say a blessing over him when he went; only her lips twitched with the pain of silence.

Long years expired before the boy returned from the strange land, a full-grown, noble youth. When Veile had her son with her again a smile played about her mouth, and for a moment it seemed as if her former beauty had enjoyed a second spring. The extraordinary ability of her son already made him famous. Wheresoever he went people were delighted with his beauty, and admired the modesty of his manner, despite such great scholarship.

The next Sabbath the young disciple of the Talmud, scarcely twenty years of age, was to demonstrate the first marks of this great learning.

The people crowded shoulder to shoulder in this great synagogue. Curious glances were cast through the lattice-work of the women's gallery above upon the dense throng. Veile occupied one of the foremost seats. She could see everything that took place below. Her face was extremely pale. All eyes were turned towards her—the mother, who was permitted to see such a day for her son! But Veile did not appear to notice what was happening before her. A weariness, such as she had never felt before, even in her greatest suffering, crept over her limbs. It was as if she must sleep during her son's address. He had hardly mounted the stairs before the ark of the laws—hardly uttered his first words—when a remarkable change crossed her face. Her cheeks burned. She arose. All her vital energy seemed aroused. Her son meanwhile was speaking down below. She could not have told what he was saying. She did not hear him—she only heard the murmur of approbation, sometimes low, sometimes loud, which came to her ears from the quarters of the men. The people were astonished at the noble bearing of the speaker, his melodious speech, and his powerful energy. When he stopped at certain times to rest it seemed as if one were in a wood swept by a storm. She could now and then hear a few voices declaring that such a one had never before been listened to. The women at her side wept; she alone could not. A choking pain pressed from her breast to her lips. Forces were astir in her heart which struggled for expression. The whole synagogue echoed with buzzing voices, but to her it seemed as if she must speak louder than these. At the very moment her son had ended she cried out unconsciously, violently throwing herself against the lattice-work:

"God! Living God! Shall I not now speak?" A dead silence followed this outcry. Nearly all had recognized this voice as that of the "silent woman." A miracle had taken place!

"Speak! Speak!" resounded the answer of the rabbi from the men's seats below. "You may now speak!"

But no reply came. Veile had fallen back into her seat, pressing both hands against her breast. When the women sitting beside her looked at her they were terrified to find that the "silent woman" had fainted. She was dead! The unsealing of her lips was her last moment.

Long years afterwards the rabbi died. On his death-bed he told those standing about him this wonderful penance of Veile.

Every girl in the gasse knew the story of the "silent woman."